Walt Disney's
Lucky Puppy

GROLIER
BOOKS

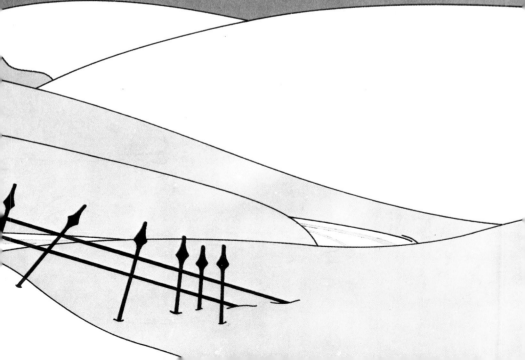

Lucky Puppy and his family
were watching the news on TV.
Something bad had happened.
The queen's jewels
had been stolen.
And the police
had not caught the thieves.

"We must find the jewels!"
said Pongo, the father.

"But how?" asked Lucky.

"We will send a message to all the dogs
in the city," he said. "Maybe someone
has seen the thieves."

Pongo and Lucky stood in the window.
And Pongo sent a message.
"A howl, a growl, and a yelp!
The queen needs your help.
Her jewels have been stolen, bow-wow!
Help us find them now."

Then Lucky began to bark, too.
"Bow-wow.
Help us find
the thieves
NOW!"

Soon every dog in the city
was barking.
The message passed
from dog to dog.
In no time at all, it had
traveled to the dogs who lived
outside the city.

In an old barn
outside the city there lived a dog
named Colonel and a cat named Sergeant Tibbs.
They heard all the barking from the city.

"What is that?" asked the Colonel.

"It is a message," said Tibbs.
"Someone has stolen the queen's jewels."

"Let's look in the empty house
on the hill," the Colonel said.

Tibbs got onto the Colonel's back
and off they went.

Before long the Colonel and Tibbs
came to the old house.

The sky was dark, but the moon
was out.

As Tibbs and the Colonel got closer
they knew someone was in the house.

A light was shining from one window.

The Colonel and Tibbs also heard
strange noises.

Tibbs and the Colonel peeked in the window.
They saw the two Baden brothers,
Horace and Jasper.
They also saw a bald man
who was playing a bass fiddle.

"Something is wrong here,"
whispered Tibbs. "Those two brothers
always mean trouble. Remember how
they stole all those dogs?"

A few minutes late[r]
Horace and Jasper
drove away in a car
with the fiddler.

"Quick," said Tibbs, "let's search the house[.]
They found an open cellar
window and sneaked inside.

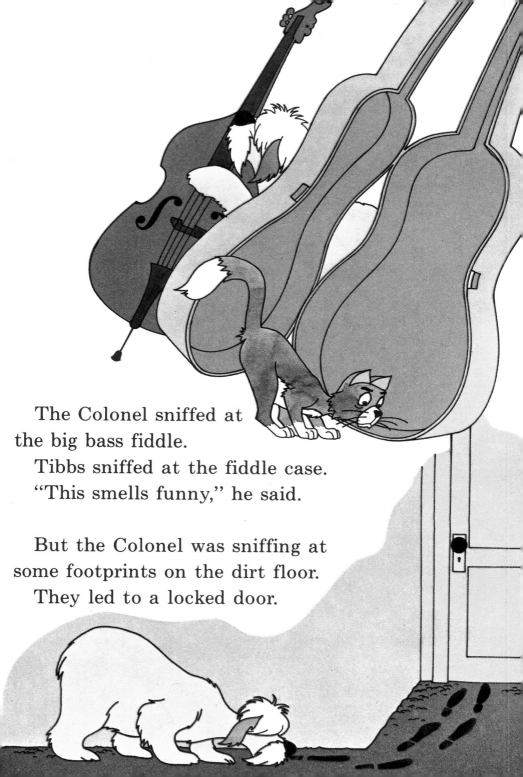

The Colonel sniffed at
the big bass fiddle.

Tibbs sniffed at the fiddle case.
"This smells funny," he said.

But the Colonel was sniffing at
some footprints on the dirt floor.
They led to a locked door.

"How can we get in?" asked Tibbs.
"We will send for Pongo," said the Colonel.
"He will know just what to do."

The Colonel and Tibbs raced back to the barn.

The Colonel sent
a message to Pongo:
"Woof, woof, woof!
Bow, wow, wow!
We need Pongo's
help right now."

The message
passed
from dog to dog.

Soon Pongo and Lucky
heard it.
"The Colonel needs
our help," said Pongo.

The next morning, Pongo and Lucky
arrived at the barn.

"Isn't that pup too small to help us?"
asked the Colonel.

"He is not too small to learn
about danger," said Pongo. "Let's hurry
to the old house."

When they got there, Pongo and
his friends peeked in the window.
    They did not see anyone.
    Lucky tried to peek, too.
    But he was too small.
    "Maybe the cellar window
is still open," said Tibbs.

The window WAS open, and Pongo went in first.

The Colonel, Tibbs, and Lucky
followed Pongo down the stairs.

At the bottom
of the stairs,
they stopped at
the locked door.

Pongo began to dig a hole.
He wanted to get under the door.
The Colonel and Tibbs watched.
Lucky Puppy watched, too.
The hole grew bigger and bigger.
But it was still not big enough
for Pongo.

"*I* can get through
that hole, Dad,"
said Lucky.
"Good boy!"
said Pongo.

The puppy wriggled
under the door.

Soon he wriggled
out again.

"Look at what I found!"
he cried.

Around his neck
was a diamond bracelet.

In his mouth
was a pearl necklace.

Lucky Puppy had found
the queen's jewels!

"Good work, Lucky,"
said Pongo.

Pongo told Lucky to put the jewels back.

"I will go to get the police," he said.
"As soon as Lucky comes out of the locked room,
get away from the house. Horace
and Jasper will soon be back."

Then Pongo ran all the way
to the city.

He stopped every dog
he saw along the way.
    "Bring me a policeman,"
he said.

The dogs went to work.
A Scotty knocked over
a policeman to get his attention.

A collie grabbed a motorcycle policeman.

A poodle barked
at the Chief of Police.

Soon all the dogs and all the policemen
in the city were standing around Pongo.

Pongo pointed in the direction
of the old house.

"By George!" said the Chief.
"He wants us to follow him."

By this time, Horace and Jasper had
come back to the house.

They were listening to the fiddler.

Suddenly the fiddler stopped playing.

He had heard a strange sound in the cellar.

"Go see what it is," he said.

Horace and Jasper hurried
to the cellar.

They saw the Colonel
and Tibbs.

"A dog!" shouted Jasper.

"A cat!" shouted Horace.

"Colonel!" said Tibbs.
"We can't let them
find Lucky Puppy!"

Tibbs jumped onto Horace's head.
He started hissing and spitting,
clawing and scratching.

Horace ran around and around.
"OH! OH! OH!" he screamed.

The Colonel jumped on Jasper's chest.
Jasper fell down with a crash.
"Help! Help!" he cried.

Suddenly Pongo arrived with the police.
"What is going on here?" asked the Chief.
"NOTHING! NOTHING!"
said Horace and Jasper.

But Pongo pointed
to the locked door.

The policemen broke down the door.

There was Lucky Puppy, guarding the queen's jewels.
"By George!" said the Chief. "He has found the jewels!"

A policeman put handcuffs
on Horace and Jasper.

Then the Chief checked the jewels.

"The pearl necklace is here," he said,
"but the emerald tiara is missing!"

Suddenly
Tibbs remembered
the fiddler.
He raced
up the stairs...

and sniffed inside
the open
fiddle case.

But the fiddler had heard
the police in the cellar.
He put on his jacket and
slammed the fiddle case shut.
"MEOW! MEOW!" screeched Tibbs
from inside the fiddle case.

The fiddler began to run.
But he did not run fast enough.

The police heard
Tibbs screeching.
They caught
the fiddler and
put handcuffs
on him.

The policemen led
the fiddler, Jasper, and
Horace into the police van.

"Open the fiddle case," said the Chief.
There sat Tibbs with something green
and shiny on his head.
"By George!" said the Chief.
"It's the emerald tiara!"

The next evening
the whole family was watchin[g]
the news on television again.
Lucky Puppy's happy face
appeared on the screen.
He was a hero
because he had found
the queen's jewels.